To: Maria & Nathan,

Great Niece & Great Nephew
in Tonkawa, OK.

Blessings.

Tom Roberts
2012

The Little Lost Sock

a story by Tom Roberts

illustrated by Jim Brummond

THE LITTLE LOST SOCK
Text copyright © 2011 by Tom Roberts
Illustration copyright © 2011 by Jim Brummond
Printed in the U.S.A. All rights reserved.

TnT Publushing
Sioux Falls, SD 57103

Photography, Illustration and Design
by Jim Brummond
Brummond Photo and Design
www.jimbrummond.com
art@jimbrummond.com

Printed by Maximum Graphics
1245 Lakeview Drive
Chaska, MN 55318-9506
Maximum Graphics, Minneapolis, MN
Job # 48580
Press Date: July 2011
Printed on Gusto® 100 lb. satin text paper

ISBN 978-0-9723868-3-8

I dedicate this story to all my Christian friends out there
who make an effort to help the little lost socks of the world.

Tom Roberts

"A faithful friend is the medicine of life."

- Ecclesiastes 6:16

THE LITTLE LOST SOCK

I must admit that while writing this story I had the kids at Children's Home Society in mind. Little lost socks who often come from a world filled with tragic circumstances where those around them are just as adrift and are in need of help. But, since then I've begun to realize that there are many others who fit this description. At one time or another I think many of us have experienced an episode in our lives when we feel a little lost and in need of a good friend.

I for one am very grateful for all the Christian friends in my life who have helped me whenever I have struggled. Friends who are always there to listen without judgment and provide reassurance that I am loved. Friends who remind me that I have it inside me to be better. Friends who remind me that God cares and that a little faith and effort can go a long way in making a positive difference.

Tom Roberts

But there among the jumble
Near a toy wooden block
Is the subject of this story
A little scarlet sock

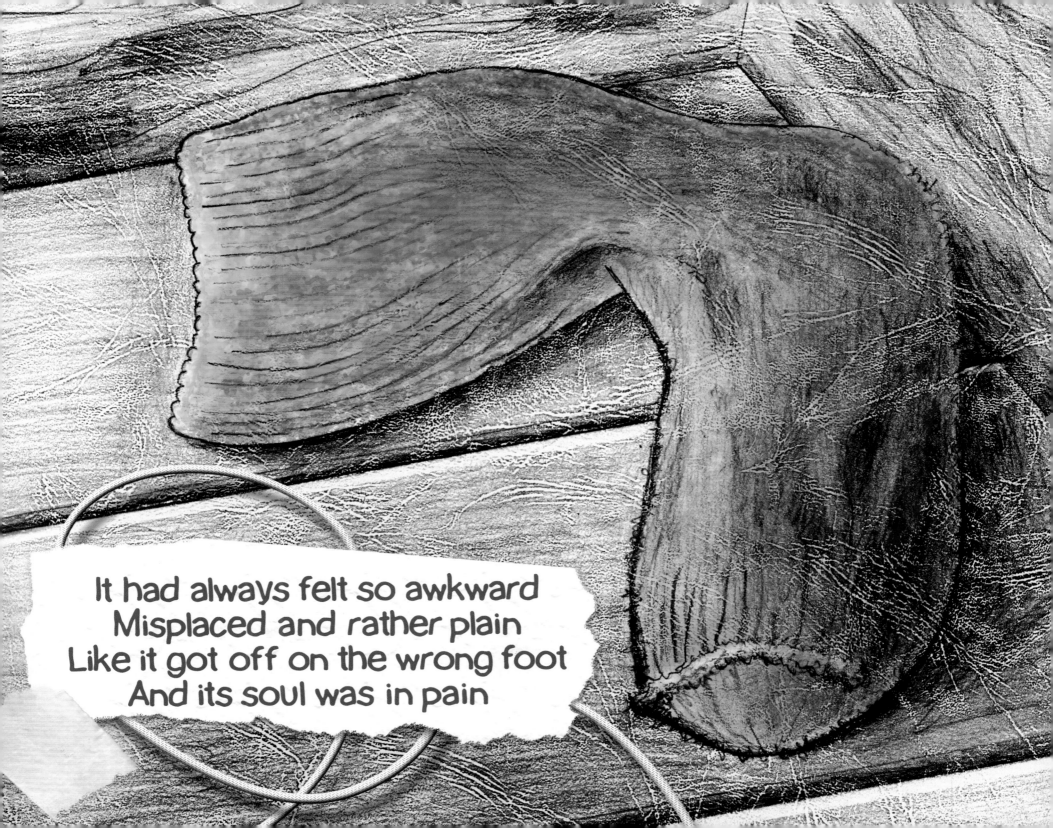

It had always felt so awkward
Misplaced and rather plain
Like it got off on the wrong foot
And its soul was in pain

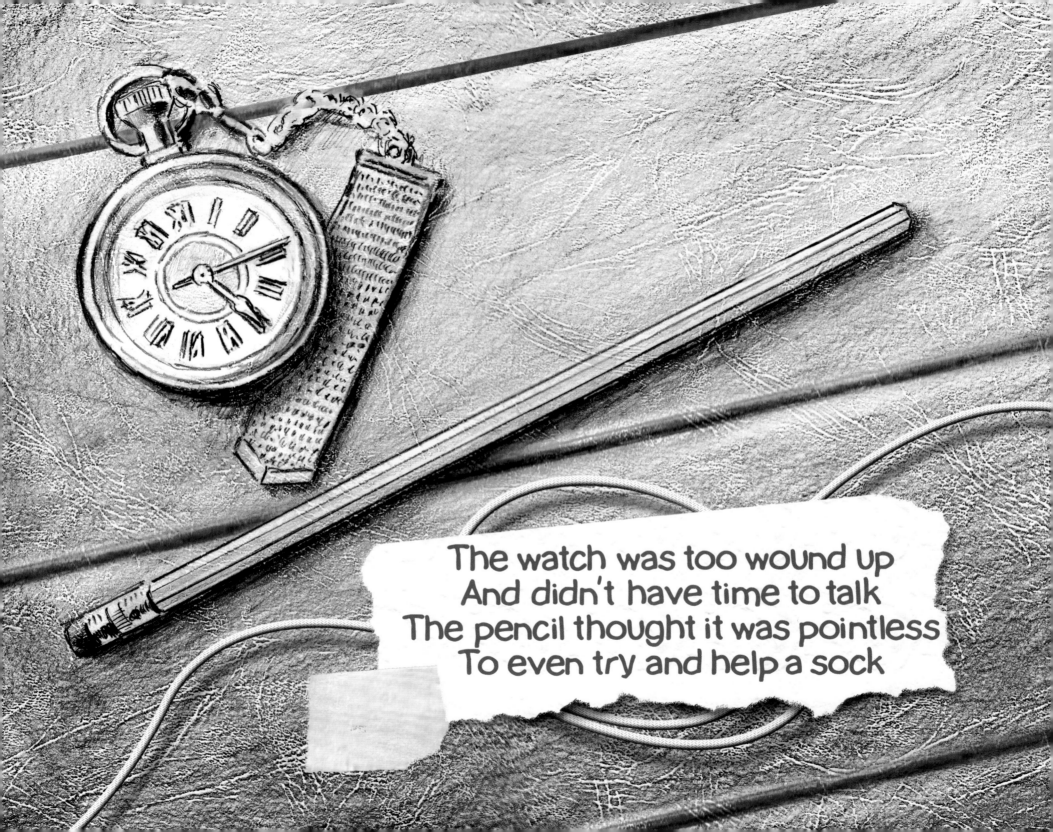

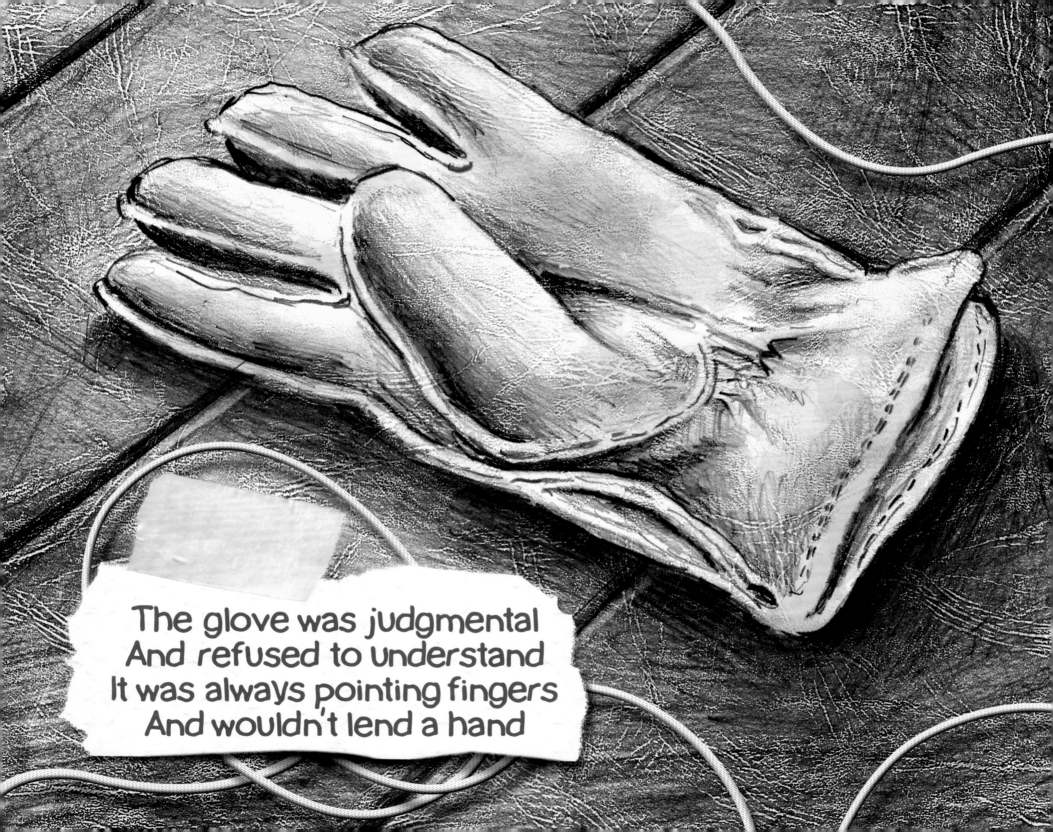

The hat was self absorbed
About the lofty life it lead
Yet it was always complaining
That it couldn't get ahead

The brick was much the same
And quit trying in an instant
It's as if it hit a wall
And the odds were stacked against it

Neither the matchbox nor the candle
Nor the lantern could shed some light

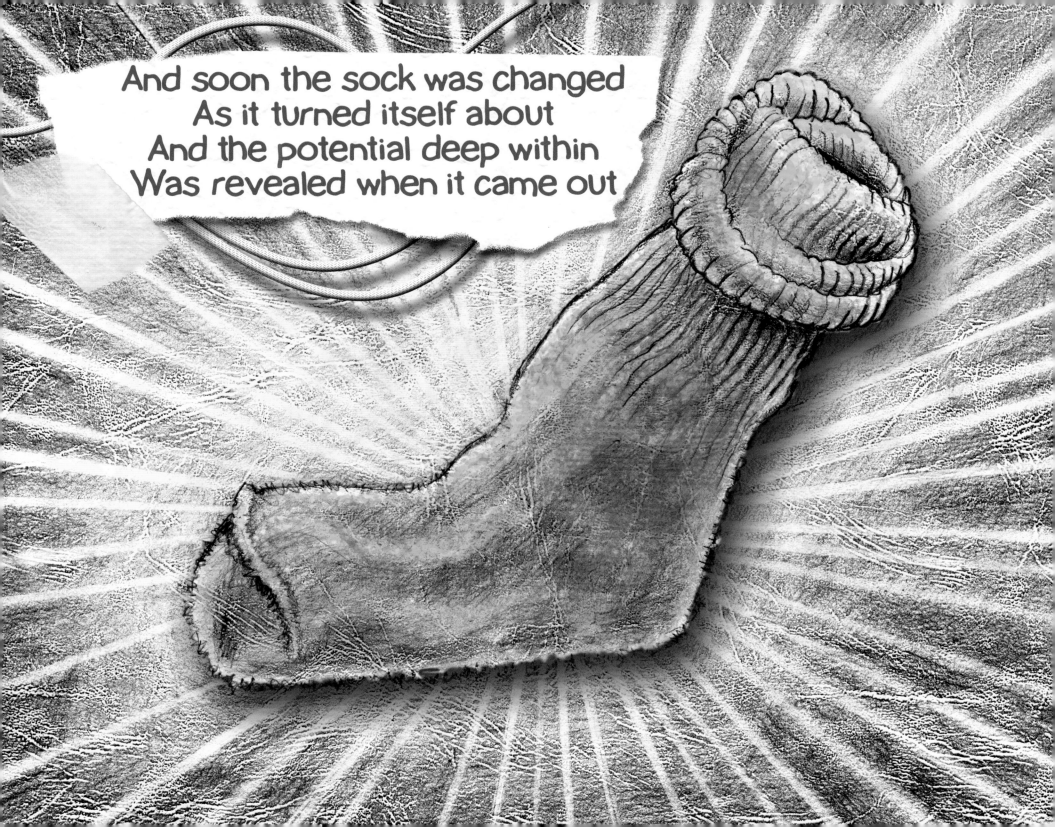

"Every tattered scrap has a story to share –
- deserving our attention, our support and care."

- Tom Roberts

CHILDREN'S HOME SOCIETY

With a history spanning more than a century, Children's Home Society (CHS) is the oldest human service agency in South Dakota. Pioneer child advocates Elizabeth and William Sherrard moved to South Dakota in 1890, and soon became determined to help the growing number of abused and abandoned children in the region. By welcoming those first children into their own home in 1893, Children's Home Society was born. The Sherrards were also instrumental in writing the first child protection laws for the state of South Dakota.

Today Children's Home Society serves over 2,000 children each year through residential treatment, education, emergency shelter, forensic interview centers, foster care and adoption programs, relative placements, and prevention services. The majority of the children are ages 4-13, and many are victims of abuse and/or neglect.

Services are provided through Black Hills Children's Home, just southwest of Rapid City; Sioux Falls Children's Home in Sioux Falls; and Children's Inn in Sioux Falls.

An agency proud of its Christian heritage, Children's Home Society continues to reflect both the vision and the compassion of the Sherrards. We appreciate all the prayers that are lifted up for the children here. Our prayer is that these children will always be surrounded by love, and be provided the guidance and opportunity to reach their God-given potential.

www.chssd.org/books